This book belongs to

17/7/23

....

....

EGMONT

We bring stories to life

Special thanks to Ian McCue and Micaela Winter
Special thanks also to Dr Deborah Weber
Written by Nancy Parent
Illustrated by Luigi Aimè, Tomatofarm

First published in Great Britain 2018 by Egmont UK Limited,
The Yellow Building, 1 Nicholas Road, London W11 4AN

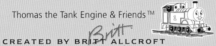

Thomas the Tank Engine & Friends™

CREATED BY BRITT ALLCROFT

ISBN 978 1 4052 8904 7

67991/1

Printed in Estonia

THOMAS & FRIENDS™

TROUBLE ON THE TRACKS

A story about sharing

The sun was shining on the Island of Sodor and the engines at Tidmouth Sheds were getting ready for a Really Useful day.

Percy was to collect all the Postal Workers and take them to an important meeting at the Post Office. But Percy had a problem.

"Percy doesn't have any passenger coaches," said Henry.

"No," said James, "but Thomas does."

So Percy asked Thomas if he could borrow Annie and Clarabel.

Thomas frowned. He did not want to share his coaches.

"What am I going to do now?" asked Percy.

Thomas could see that his friend was worried. "But Annie and Clarabel belong with me," he explained.

Percy chuffed away in a huff, leaving Thomas behind.

Suddenly an idea flew into Thomas' funnel.
"Wait for me, Percy!" he called, puffing after his friend.

Soon Thomas caught up. "I want to feel Really Useful today," he began. "Since I always pull Annie and Clarabel, why not let me take the Postal Workers to the meeting?"

"But that's supposed to be my job," said Percy. After all, he did pull the Mail Train.

Percy puffed his pistons and chuffed off again.
He was really cross now.

Thomas felt sad that his friend was upset.

"I would feel Really Useful if Percy would let me pull the Mail Train one day," he thought. "I bet if I lend Annie and Clarabel to Percy, he'll tell me I can pull it sometime."

Thomas puffed off to tell his friend. But when he explained, Percy did not want to share.

Back at Tidmouth Sheds, the two engines complained.

"Thomas won't share his coaches," said Percy.

"And Percy won't share the Mail Train," Thomas added.

Now both engines were unhappy and cross with each other.

"Humph," puffed James. "Someone should have asked *me* to take the Postal Workers to the meeting. After all, I'm the Really Splendid Engine."

"The job calls for a speedy train, and I'm the fastest one here," said Gordon.

Then Emily thought of the terrible storm that had wrecked
Tidmouth Sheds last year. "Thomas," she said, "do you remember?
Before the sheds were rebuilt, I *shared* mine with you."

Thomas and Percy looked down at their buffers sheepishly.

"Well," said Emily, "that's just what friends do. They *share*."

"Cinders and ashes, you're right!" said Thomas.

"And we're best friends," added Percy, "so we really **should** share!"

Finally, Thomas agreed to share Annie and Clarabel with Percy, and Percy agreed to let Thomas pull the Mail Train very soon.

"Thanks, Emily!" the two engines called as
they puffed off to find Thomas' coaches.

Meanwhile, Annie and Clarabel were waiting at Knapford Station.

"I do hope Thomas gets here soon," said Clarabel.

Just then, Thomas and Percy puffed into the station.

"Annie and Clarabel," Thomas began, "Percy needs help bringing the Postal Workers to an important meeting today. He has asked to borrow you both, and I said I would ask you because I want to share."

"Well, of course," said Annie cheerfully.

"Yes," agreed Clarabel. "Annie and I were hoping to be Really Useful today."

So Percy set off with Annie and Clarabel, and together they took everyone to the meeting. Percy was a very happy little green engine!

Percy puffed excitedly when he got back to the station.
"I've agreed to give Thomas a turn at pulling the Mail
Train on the next run. I want to share, too."

"Hooray!" cheered Annie and Clarabel.

The next day, Percy and the coaches watched as Thomas was coupled to the Mail Train.

"You two are caring, sharing friends," said Annie.

"Sharing is being Really Useful!" Thomas peeped happily.

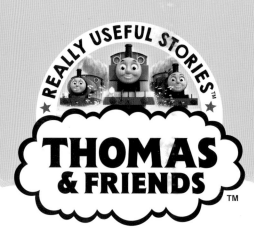

THOMAS & FRIENDS™

REALLY USEFUL STORIES™

Really Useful Stories™ can help children talk about new experiences. Here are some questions about this story that can help you talk about friendship and sharing.

Does Thomas have a best friend? Do you?

When Percy asked if he could borrow Annie and Clarabel, what do you think Thomas should have said?

When Thomas said no to Percy, how did that make Percy feel?

How did sharing make Thomas and Percy feel?

Why do you think it's important to share?